Gravity: Em

By Dominic Morgan
Chaos Nation Theory

To Reader with Love

D morgan

ISBN 978-1-71694-228-0

Dedication: Dear Fallen

This page is dedicated to those who passed away. You will always be in our hearts and never forgotten. Rest in peace and see you again one day.

Dorothy Elaine Wynter (06 June 1991), Dominic James Taylor (19 July 1991), Leanora Taylor (19 March 1993), Wilfred Simpson (20 October 2004), Arden Morgan, (11 March 2009), Clay Wynter, (10 September 2009), Joana Honger, Lindon Browne (31 July 2016) Evelyn Trotman (09 March 2019) and Dawn Reynolds (09 April 2020).

To all those who I have forgotten to add and didn't mention may you also rest in peace.

Contents

For every heart that finds a love,
There is a heart that cries.
For every dream that is reborn,

My Sister's name is Dorothy Wynter
She's one year older, she's born in September
It's surprising to see how patient she'd be

I can't explain it, but what I saw must have been a dream, as if it was not real or what could be my future, but anyway, this was my dream.

Introduction: Empty Spaces
(20/10/15)

This is from a man, who's written so much, came so far and achieved a fair amount, but yet all my greatest writing has come from lost emotions and pain from within. Not all my work has come from it, but a lot has and that has kept me connected with so many.

My words have become an inspiration for others and I believe I have used them well. I've used and thought about how to connect with the readers so much that every story, not every chapter tells a story. Whether I was writing for someone else or for me, my words have touched someone but at last, I still feel this pain.

My way with words has been described as a genius but I've always believed that geniuses become eccentrics or so but perhaps with me, I'm more of the arrant type, either way, I will continue to write cause this is what I do and I seem to be good at it.

My creativeness comes from the Lord God who encourages me to write. My inspiration comes from anything, including pain because someone may be going through something and I could help. I've written about many things and intern that I hope that will help them. I hope I touch a life or be an inspiration. I'd know I'd feel good if my words encouraged someone.

I often wonder why my pain and emptiness becomes my greatest tool for connecting. I haven't a clue I just know that while I have something to say or am able to connect with the world this way I will have a purpose. As long as someone needs me or rather what I have to say I shall continue to write. Thank you, God, for these abilities.

So my Joy, my pain, my emptiness and even my inspiration become not only my greatest weakness but also my greatest strength and although I wish it to be different I'm glad I have a place on this earth and God has blessed me with something. It may be small but it's mine.

These books will be my legacy. The proof I once existed and will become my biggest gift to this earth. My words, my life, my joy, my happiness and my pain will be my greatest strength and also my weakness.

This book contains thoughts, Poems, Mini Stories and Stories of a non-specific thoughts. These are a blank canvas type designs. Though they are of such nature, some are personal thoughts. This is my Empty Space.

Chapter I: Hate Is A Burden
(28/09/15)

Hate is a burden which Stains the earth

When those with the warm heart are taken advantage of
because of their nature,
Hate is a burden which stains the earth.

When those who are treated like their rights do not matter,
Hate is a burden which stains the earth.

When good fathers are treated the same as the bad fathers,
Hate is a burden which stains the earth.

When good fathers are treated like they have no rights to
their children,
Hate is a burden which stains the earth.

When the parents who abused the children get to keep their
kids and those who work their hardest to be good parents
loses their children,
Hate is a burden which stains the earth.

When you see the people, who don't care get rewarded well,
Hate is a burden which stains the earth.

When you say you may need help then people take it for
weaknesses or someone who can't do the job,
Hate is a burden which stains the earth.

When the pain of loss or sadness grows,
Hate is a burden which stains the earth.

When men earn more than women and women having to
fight harder than men for their rights.
Hate is a burden which rules the earth.

When your trust is broken by a loved one, friend or family,
Hate is a burden which stains the earth.

When your heart is broken beyond repair,
Hate is the beginning which rules your heart

When there is nothing left of a person's humanity,
Hate is a substance which rules the earth.

Love is sometimes blind and Hate rules,
Hate will always be this burden when carried causes
problems of its own, still, it rules the earth.

Chapter II: For The One He Loved
(07/10/15)

A man who gave himself for love was left to weep in pain,
He gave it all for the one he loved but surely has regrets.
He did all he can and even more and the sacrifices he would make,
To give it all for that one moment, that moment he could feel loved, happy and to see his dreams unfold

Be it, family, friend or enemies it didn't matter if they got in the way, it was all the same.
To search for the love so pure and true, that love that grows and grows
The price he paid was and is high, himself in exchange for it all

He sat under the tree on a starry night wondering what he should do,

The sacrifice was high but also knew what he had to do.
He had to keep pushing himself past his limits so he thought while sitting under the tree

"You know what," he said as sat there thinking under the tree, "I shall work so hard to make her happy, give her what she needs not wants and then I'll become happy as her joy will make me happy".
But forgot the one basic truth that the only way to be truly happy comes from the joy and love from within.

Chapter III: A Mother's Love
(14/10/15)

I, you're, mother has adored you since the day you were born, actually, to be exact, since before you were born. You are my pride, my greatest joy in life and I will always love you till the end of time and no matter what you do, this will never change.

Since I learnt of my pregnancy, I couldn't wait to see you. Whether you are a boy or girl It doesn't matter to me as you, my baby I can't wait to hold. Oh the joy you're bringing me I must say is huge and so amazing and the only thing that can top this is the day I hold you for the first time, then the greatest moment of my life will be confirmed.

I didn't know how much in love with you I would become. Don't get me wrong I was hugely in love with you from before but now my love for you has intensified, so much to the point where it borders over into the possessive stages but I'm a first-time mother what more would you expect.

I can't wait for you to be born, to see those little toes kick all about, to feel your tiny hands, to see your little face, too hear you cry but more importantly to feel you close to me and to hold you for the first time.

Of course, I'd be lying if I didn't say I'm looking forward to the pains I'm going to have giving birth or the sleepless nights, but with pain comes the joy of birth and the proudest parent moments that trumps every and anything that has come before.

When you are born, I will shower you with all my love when I see you. I will not put you down. I will give you all my joy, my passion, my heart and my time oh and don't forget those dodgy pictures and there will be loads of those. Don't worry there will be thousands of others too, on a file I'll save them, the one under your name or I shall call it "The Greatest Gift From God".

You are God's work at his finest. The beginning of life, the joys of life and my greatest reward from God. The pinnacle of my life and my chance for true hope and happiness. The proof that I really do have a purpose on this earth and my reason for living. The greatest person (can't call you thing) I will ever have oh did I ramble too much well you get the picture I hope but to make you understand, my heart, love, time and the rest of my life are yours.

Well, that's me for done for today because I need to buy food for us, and this is only day one. You have the rest of the term of the pregnancy to hear me praise you for all the joys you will give me. I shall sign off by crying happily but only until tonight and tomorrow. I'll enjoy the kicking for the time will fly and I will see you soon.

Chapter IV: His Woeful Sorrow!!
(30/10/15)

Today I feel sadness and sorrow in heart,
For I have something to lose.
I try and try and work so hard,
Because I always have something to prove.

Every day my joy feels short-lived
When I think about everything that can go wrong.
But tomorrow is another day,
Still another day in which I must be strong.

Every day I hope will be a new day,
And that I'll make it through without feeling depleted.
But all I seem to find is many ways,
Yes, many many ways in which I can be defeated.

All I have is empty dreams, broken promises and words
that's so untrue.
At times I can't help feeling, maybe I did someone wrong and
this wrath is overdue.
Still, if it's true and this is all due,
I hope to God, pray to God, I make it through.

One day I know I'll wake, and this will all be a dream.
A bad dream but not as tough as it seems.
Or it won't and I'll ask God to take my soul,
Cause my life is full of screams.
But until I'm done and had enough and can't rise to fight any
more.

I'll keep fighting, and I pray, no matter what happens, I'll always fight for the cause.

All I have is the material stuff I surround myself with, cause that's all I ever know.
I still do this every day, I count the days my heart never grew.
So until the day where I can say I'm free of pain and all these empty sorrows.
Happiness and joy, are just words, nothing more nothing less,
Words that I can only borrow.

Chapter V: A Sincere Heart
(11/11/15)

Every moment I'm with you,
Is one I truly cherish.
Every moment we spend apart and not together,
My heart is sure to perish.

I want to show you off to the world,
You're the apple of my eyes.
Our love is one that grows and is true,
One which can never be despised.

Even moments we are together,
I have no doubt that it is true,
All the voices including my own will always say,
Yes my heart, now and forever will always say, I Love you.

I know that when I look at you,
Makes me proud that I know you.
All these feelings inside, I hold with pride,
Cause I know that they are true

The Joy, happiness and love we share it and that you give,
are ones that I love.
These are strong feelings deep within,
Ones from God above.

I pray this day will never come,
The day we have to part.
The cause will surely be the day,
The day I lose my heart.

I will cherish all the memories,
Like they were my last.
And share you all my new ones,
I know this joy will last.

Chapter VI: I am, Who I am
(19.11.15)

I am, who I am,
For I am unique and an individual
Built with dreams and ambitions
A gift from God
For I am me.

I am special to those who need and want me
I am loved for those who care for me
I am treasured by those who admire me
And I am despised by those who hate me
But I'll still be me

Sometimes I'm happy and sometimes I'm angry
Sometimes laugh and sometimes I'm mad
Sometimes I love and sometimes I hate
Sometimes I'm confident and sometimes I'm nervous
Sometimes I'm giving and sometimes I'm Jealous

Sometimes I have faith and sometimes I don't
Sometimes I believe and sometimes I don't
Sometimes I have the courage and sometimes I have to
discourage
Sometimes I tell the truth and sometimes I lie

I tried once to be who I could be and failed with every
attempt
For I wasn't happy to be me

I tried to be someone else to rid myself of the flaws and to be
free
But this could never work for I wouldn't be me
I hope I can be loved for me as me
Many people will try to come against me, for me being me
I will always work to do my best and remember I'm free to be
me
I pray I never become too discouraged for me being me
For this is who I'm meant to be and show, for everyone to
see
I will shine brightly as the sun, one day I will know
God will lead my path, that I definitely know

So yes I am, that I am
For I am unique and an individual
For I'm proud to be me
For I am a human, and God does love me

Chapter VII: The Knowing (Trapped In Hell) (25/11/15)

This is a poem about the knowing,
So listen close to all who are growing,
We're trapped in our own hell.

When people versus people,
No one is equal,
Then get annoyed when there is a sequel.

We live in a world which is so demanding,
The government controls our understanding,
All nations are divided and self commanding,
We live together with no understanding.

Still, We Live In This Hell.

Our ignorance in society,
Makes us blissful in our reality,
We can not afford to just wait for change,
To wait only serves to create hate,
For we as people must learn to play it straight,
To find ourselves in this world, but we first must change.

We're the beauty of God's creations,
But remain divided into different nations,
We the shiver-less society,
Attacks the people who chose a variety,
How can this be?

Still, We Created This Hell.

This hell on earth,
Is the vision the devil has given birth,
In conflict and chaos but that's not the worst,
We rape, stone, conquer, kill, oppress our people,
So tell me how are we equal.

We try as a society attempt to pursue our vision,
But we are just like crabs, only division,
Is that really a decision or,
Based on religion.

For in God we trust,
Cause There is no us,
In flesh, we lust,
By choice by us.

Still, We Live In Our Own Hell.

Through the use of knowledge, we cover our basic needs,
Yet we pursue all things wrong because of wealth and greed,
And in life, this is how we wanna succeed,
Best believe.

We lust after others,
That belongs to or brothers,
Always causing a fuss,
When it happens to us.

Still, We Trapped In Our Own Hell

We let the courts decided our fate,
We never seem to congregate,

Even in situations where we can relate,
How deep was our hate?
We like to segregate.

Still we here for today and maybe tomorrow,
We must remember that time is borrowed,
For these are trials which are put to test us,
So, in God, we must always trust.

So, this was a poem about The Knowing,
Now it's up to you to choose to rebel,
Or remain in Trapped In Your Own Hell.

Chapter VIII: There You Are
(21/12/15)

When the day is long and I have no one to talk to, There you are.

When I needed a friend, not just a friend, but a lover and a partner, There you are.

When your face is the only thing I want to see, day or night, There you are.

Just by seeing you, you make me feel like I can do anything, There you are.

When I know that my dreams have come true, because all I have to do is look at you, There you are.

When we go to the park, hand in hand and enjoy the views, There you are.

When your company and your face is all I needed to get through the day, There you are.

God gave you to me for a reason and for that you have been a blessing, There you are.

When the days are long and narrow, and the days are hard and troubling, There you are.

For all you put up with and still stood by me, There you were.

From the people who knew me best and all those who thought they knew me, There you were.

When all I needed was a hug from you to inspire me through the day, a kiss that would make my heart melt I when I'm down, There you were.

And on the day, I was accused of something that wasn't true and all people was against me, You was still there.

No matter how far you go or where you are in the world. No matter where fate takes us or no matter how bad things may get. No matter what life may bring or even throw at us or time may do to us. I want you to know, I too will be here.

People may come and go, either by choice or by loss. They may leave us as friends and family and give us a hard time. People will put us through hell to try and split us up but they'll never succeed, We will never part.

Until the day we die, either if you go first or I go first, may we be old and grey and die of natural causes. Just like our vows, till death do us part and even when we do we shall never leave each other's side. In death shall never part. We will never part.

Our love grows and grows and forever growing, but there is one thing that will always be and never end, You was always there.

Chapter IX: The Red Rose
(21/01/16)

I am like a red rose that shines in the day and is unseen in the light. My beauty is amazing to the eye. I smell so amazing and make a wonderful gift, you'll never forget me in a hurry.

I'm the gift that keeps on giving for when people receive me, they smile, cry or is and is very grateful or I'm taken to a grave for remembrance, either way, I hope that I bring you joy.

I soak up the sun and water with ease as to me it's my source of light and the means I need to live, but I don't complain. I get it every day, especially the attention, that I really love more than anything else.

People admire my beauty from afar and even close up. They love the fact that I don't just come in red, but, my family comes in many different one's. From Blue to yellow, they are my brothers and sisters and as part of the flower family which is very big, I definitely have my work cut out for me.

I enjoy my life day by day, take it in my stride, for I don't have to find the food myself or go hunting for it, but if I'm in the wild, I wish I could, but I do have a dream to please the person that sees me more.

My gifts to the world are my amazing colours and smell, they give the means to my true beauty that shines at the end of the day, you know what and who I am. There's nothing about me which is hidden or kept out of the line of sight. I peak when my leaves are fully bloomed.

Like all good things, I will have to die and my leaves start to wither away, and I fold up. When I start to die, I start to cry for I wish I could last longer. Though my time is short I'm proud I made you smile, in with the chance I had, but I know I that when I die, I will be replaced soon thus the cycle continues.

I was for a season and not just for the day for you never forget my beauty, for all the love and joy that was shared, because of me will never ever be forgotten. I will always be a symbol of love and affection especially when words fail, I most definitely won't, a way to say sorry for the person that full of guilt and also to say on say thank you and goodbye. For all that comes before me and after me, There will only be one or a group of me.

I'm am blessed with beauty, love and loved is me and something for everyone to see, but now I'm gone and in the bin, as death it came for me, I shall always live on in the hearts but as a memory to those who I've seen.

Chapter X: In God We Trust
(22/12/14)

When life pulls you down and you need an intervention,
God's not far away through prayer and intermissions.

Maybe your heart is in pain or can't make the right decision,
Just look real deeper and try to see what God has
envisioned.

One day you'll see either today or tomorrow,
Joy and happiness will come tomorrow, through pain and
through sorrow.

Life isn't easy and people always have the stuff to say,
Put on the armour God, think peaceful, and wish them well
along there way.

We won't live forever so do your best to be strong,
Try deep in your heart, wholeheartedly, to forgive those who
did you wrong.

So I say to the things in life that you want, they won't come
cheap,
But put your mind to task in hand, look within your heart keep
digging and go deep.

For the victory is yours, through hard work and determination
and then you can weep,
These are tears of happiness, cause today you toiled,
tomorrow/soon you will reap.

Chapter XI: Crying Aloud
(15/02/15)

When I cried, I cried allowed,
From the pain, I felt,
From the betrayal that was dealt,
And for the facts I was alone.

Alone again, with me myself and pain,
With all the hurt I feel the strain.
I felt it once before,
And want to feel it no more.

I cried in my bed, deep beneath the sheets,
This pain is insane.
If this was just a cut or a bruise, it wouldn't last as long,
If It was because I lost my phone or wallet, sure I'd feel
something but I would be strong.
But this pain is of the heart, dealt by loss and betrayal and
this one will take longer.

Day by night, the moment I fight I grow weak.
This unbearable torment I feel weak,
The same today, the same tomorrow,
But still, there's time to borrow.

I cried aloud but no one heard me.
I cried in pain but no one heard me.
I cried to the public but no one heard me.
My tears for help fell in vain.

I cried till in heaps,

I cried until I could sleep,
But I know the pain will still be there tomorrow.
The feeling, it is hollow,
But I know in time that joy it will follow,
When my heart it heals again.
So for now, I sleep,
No more I weep as I leave the day behind.

I'm a shadow of my former self, but I won't be forever,
I'll try to grow strong and endeavour,
For tomorrow will be long, but I will be strong till I won't have
to cry again.

Chapter XII: I'm Sorry!!
(28/02/15)

I'm sorry I never got to be the best.
I'm sorry if I was always stressed.
I'm sorry if I was never better than the rest.
I'm sorry if I failed the test.

I'm sorry if I was the biggest fool.
I'm sorry if I was so uncool.
I'm sorry if I couldn't make you proud.
I'm sorry if I was always loud.

I'm sorry that I'm never around.
I'm sorry that I was always down.
I'm sorry for always putting myself first.
I'm sorry for always making you feel the worst.

I'm sorry to my friends and family and how I let you all down.
I'm sorry for all the bias views I express.
I'm sorry I never confessed how I fell.
I'm sorry for all the tears I shed but did it all in vain.
I'm sorry for all the pain.

Yes, I'm sorry for all the pains I've caused, the lies I've told,
the people I've hurt, the hearts I've broken.
The joy I've robbed, the backstabbing I've done, the smiles
I've stolen, and the so many people I couldn't help and the
lives I couldn't save......

Huh but wait, I'm still alive aren't I,
I'm not dead yet,

I can feel my own hand, I can feel my own heartbeat and pulse, my God I'm still alive.
So why do I talk like I can't rectify these things and my mistakes? interesting.

So I've decided, starting from right now and not tomorrow, cause tomorrow never comes if I leave it, that I will make a change.
I shall correct my past mistakes by changing things and making new ones,
Cause I'm not perfect and I prone to doing so.
I will stand up and be accounted for in whatever I do.
I shall make someone happy, by creating laughter and joy, not anger and pain.
I will always work the hardest, be there early, leave later but definitely you will see me.
I shall make everyone proud and be the best that I can be.
But, before I go to bed, I'll definitely, most definitely just be me.

Chapter XIII:
The Chaos and Corruption In This World
(02/01/15)(18/02/15)

We Live in a world:

Where hate, Lust and Greed is an everyday norm.
Where we Judge others happily but take offensive to being
Judged.

Where the weak are oppressed, The poor can't afford
anything and there are homeless people on the streets with
no food to eat.
Where one mistake destroys all the good you do.

Where we lie for the purpose to protect, hide or lie for no
reasons.
Where others enjoy causing pain, affliction, agony on others,
oppressing and controlling others.

Where some children live in fear of abuse, rape and or being
killed.
Where rape is common in certain parts of the world, other
men enjoy it and the victims are treated like the suspects.

Where domestic abuse goes unpunished.
Where people spend their lives unhappy.

Where racism is acceptable.
Where are dreams get turned into nightmares?

Where money controls the world.

Where terrorism exists.

Where people kill themselves or self-harm because they can't cope with the pressure of the world or believe they have nothing to live for.
Where good people see things but are afraid or scared to say or do anything.

Where if you have a disability, you're treated as a second class citizen, with no dignity or respect.
Where there Is such a thing as a second and third world.

Where people misuse or abuse their power/authority over others.
Where you can't practise your religion without fear of persecution or being killed.

Where affairs are justified by any means.
Where getting a job isn't easy or has discrimination.
where there are honour killings.

The worse of all is that we live in this world where all this is just another day in the world. Despite all the sadness, is still hope and good people out there that do what is the right thing like stand up for the weak and oppressed. Where they fight every day for a fairer world and still have hopes and dreams. Children of the world, we need to come together in unity and harmony to stop these things, for a better understanding and to bring peace to this world of chaos. Be the change you wish to see in this world by not being conformed of this world but being transformed in this world. We can do this by standing up for justice and doing the right thing even when faced with adversity.

Chapter XIV: In Case I Never Said It
(02/04/2020)

For every time that we met, you made me smile
For every time that we spoke on the phone, I always ran out
of things to say
For every time you texted me, my heart filled with joy
For every time you thanked me, you validated me
And for every time I didn't see or hear from you, I missed you
more than words could say.

For every hug we gave each other, I felt your warmth
For every kiss on the cheek and then later on the lips, it felt
amazing
For every time I held you in my arms, I never wanted to let go
And for every time we made love, it was always special.

Your smile could light up the room for miles
Your heart and generosity always showed when offered me
things
Your eyes although brown like mine shined like diamonds
Altogether you and all your beauty from head to toe outshone
even the Goddesses
The perfect woman in the world looks forth best compared to
you.

You have so much strength both inside and out and you
show without knowing it
You are very smart and full of wisdom from years of research
You put your everything into everything you do, you give it
heart

And no matter what comes your way you always face it down
with positivity.

I've never told you how I felt because I was so shy
I always dreamed of us together going to so many cool
places
Oh how I do enjoy your company
I will always love you forever
You are very special to me like a four-leaf clover, it's very
special, hard to find
But once I have you I Knew I never want to lose you.

Chapter XV: Dear Fallen
(14.05.16)

We carry around the dreams you had for us in our hearts, the memories we shared, all the joy and laughs we had and more importantly the time we had together. Although it was as long we would have liked it to be we still have them. Everything we been through helped shaped who I am and what I should stand for, good or bad and for that, I'm eternally grateful. You may be gone but your memories live on in our hearts forever and just because you are gone, it doesn't mean we have to forget you, your legacy lives on in All those, lives you touched and was there to be a part of. Your life started like a flower being planet being planted in the ground and with time, like you, the flower grew. Like you, the flower grew up very strong and capable of dealing with anything that came your way and from that, it showed what it was capable of. Your life also showed that as well but not am only that but time showed your character and who you was. There was never a day when you failed to show your true personality because you knew who you was and wanted to be in life. Again and again, you demonstrated this in your everyday life and how you lived, in your code, what you believed in and how you were raised. Time is a wonderful thing but also a bad thing as just as you mature and like the sunrise, so to does it set and times runs out but not without leaving everlasting memories that will remain with us. All the stories we heard and witnessed, every memory whether it be good or bad will remain with us till the day our time runs out. As flower dies, so do we or rather so did you but unlike life where there are only one means of starting life, death comes in many different ways and can come at any different time. Natural causes are defined by anything where the person wasn't killed, for example, the number one and causes of this and also the causes of more deaths than killings and can't be prosecuted is Cancer and Heart Attacks. Once the last leaf is fallen, it's time to dispose of the what remains and that's the same with the human body but with this, it's different and depending on what your choices, you can be either buried or cremated. There is always a church service to celebrate and say words of remembrance to get out how you feel about the person and final goodbyes. This is always the final chance to say goodbye to the person for when you leave the church you leave without the person you brought there in the first place because that person would either have been buried or left waiting in a crematorium waiting to be buried but the only difference is, is that with cremation is that you can return with the ashes on another. In the meantime, when you leave with the person who dies, more than often you go somewhere to a hall, where you celebrate the person's life and rejoice in that person's life, no one ever remembers the bad things they've done which are good. There will never be a person quite like the dealt departed and for that the memories are precious. Ashes to Ashes, Dust to Dust no matter how it all ends, we all have to go one day so let's raise a glass to the dearly departed and celebrate the memories and move forward.

Chapter XVI: Dedication To Dorothy Elaine Wynter (29.02.16)

For every heart that finds love,
There is a heart that cries.
For every dream that is reborn,
There is a dream that dies.

For every day that's filled with sun,
There is a day of rain.
For every hour of joy, we fill,
There is an hour of pain.

For every smile upon one's face,
There is a tear to cry.
For every fond hello we say,
There is a sad goodbye.

For every new face in the world,
There is a grave to see.
For every heart that's open wide,
There's one without a key.

When I lie down, I will not be afraid
Yes, I shall lie down, and my sleep will be sweet.

In Loving Memory Of
Dorothy Elaine Wynter
25 Sept 1963 - 06 June 1991

Chapter XVII: Dorothy (Sessions By Valerie Simpson) (08.03.16

My Sister's name is Dorothy Wynter
She's one year older, she's born in September
It's surprising to see how patient she'd be
Especially when she's so patient with me
She is good at judo and she's got her black belt
I am sitting here wondering how she felt
When she sings to me she sounds so nice
She sings to me and Rema and we take her advice
She's the best sister I'll ever know
Because here and Rema was around to watch me grow.

**In Loving Memory Of
Dorothy Elaine Wynter
25 Sept 1963 - 06 June 1991**

Chapter XVIII: Shane Winters: Prospects Of The Future
(11/12/15)

I can't explain it but what I saw must have been a dream, as if it was not real or what could be my future. Anyway, this was my dream. The day was a rather cloudy day, it was raining, and I had just finished work. I worked as a trouble consultant in London, who helped anyone with personal issues and problems and enjoyed the work I did.

The Perfect Vision

One day, I must have gone to the library to study on psychology when (well I wasn't paying attention) I bumped into the Liberian. I don't know what came over me but I felt like I must have fallen in love. I apologized for my clumsiness and asked her name. She said her name was Emerly Stepherson and she told me her occupation was a part-time Liberian who worked Monday, Tuesdays and Fridays and on the other days she worked in a baker's shop. She had nice brown hair, blue eyes, snow-white skin and a smile to die for. It was as if an angel had fallen out of heaven or as if my prayers had been answered there and then.

The Liberians Life

She described herself as a laid back person with a simple ambition and with one goal, to be a famous author one day and was in the middle of writing a book. She described her family as also being laid back and well dressed. Her mum is a lawyer and her dad a sales manager. They met on board a ship on their way to the Bahamas where they fell in love. She said that she went to university in Oxford and had got her degree in business studies and English language. I don't know what attracted me to her, maybe it was that she could think for herself, she was intelligent or that she reminded me of Sharon Alton but whatever it was the other good thing is she was single.

The Parents

After that day we kept in close contact and was talking on the days we can and at the library. It was Friday, I got the guts together and asked her out on a date and she said yes. I went to her house that night to pick her up, I wore a kind of suit, without the blazer and with a pair of well-polished shoes. I got to the house where she was living, she lived with her parents. Growing up her parents were strict in her upbringing but anyway, the house was fairly big and the front garden had a tree and daffodils. As I got to the door, I felt kind of nervous about the meeting the parents but when she appeared my nerves went down and I felt at ease, a bit. I went into the house her parents had their own conservatory right near the dining room area at the back of the house, that's where her mum worked all the cases, she was a lawyer. The conservatory had loads of law books, some old and some new and her parents had leather sofas in the front room. I sat down, I had a drink and then in came the parents. I didn't know what to expect so I got tense again but Emerly claimed me down and told me to relax and to be myself. Her dad was American and her mum is British. Her dad then said to me "not to be nervous" then what came next was what I would call the Spanish

Inquisition began. The questions were where do you work? Where did I live?, what college I attended?, and what do I have planned for the future?. When the interview with the parents was over we left the house and I took Emerly to a lovely restaurant in Central London, where we got to talk and to know each other a little more.

The British Dream

I've heard it is harder to ask a woman out on a date, but even harder to build the guts and propose to one. So after a few months (7 to be exact), I found the courage to propose to Emerly. It was two months before valentines day as well which was excellent for my plans to work. It was on one of our dates where I sprung the surprise question on her. As you could imagine she was shocked but amazed at the same time but her answer was yes, which made me really happy so I sprung another surprise on Emerly, by telling her it was arranged for valentines day and the honeymoon where we would be going was to the Canaries. I had been planning this for a while with the anticipation of her saying yes and even to the point that I never consider she could say no but I knew how she felt about me so I knew she'd say yes.

The Long Road

I got together with my best friend and best man and planned out how I wanted it and what needs to be done to the point where I thought or rather knew I had it all under control. Me and Emerly had been out shopping for the rings, taking a look at cakes and getting catering sorted on other days. The days we weren't together I was with my friends looking for suits and she was out buying wedding and bridesmaids dresses. There were days where we couldn't agree on what to buy or what we wanted but we managed to work it out. It was just two weeks away from the day and I was in the middle of buying a house. Preparations for the wedding was almost done and even throughout what was to happen with the invites and the paying for the reception. Me and Emerly got through it and before we knew it the time had flown. Two weeks had gone and the glorious day was one day away.

The Light At The End Of The Tunnel

The day had come, I was at my mum's house that night. I thought I would spend some time with her before the time came to say goodbye. I was already ready to go, my mum and sister's Tara and Sharon went on ahead of me to get to the church and all that was left was for me to get my stuff together and go. Me and the best man went down to the church but we had trouble trying to get to there as there was traffic. At the church my friends, mum, sisters, dad was there, weirdly enough Emerly as well had arrived before and her family and friends were there in the church. Everything was ready but i was still stuck in traffic. Eventually we got there and I had to run in. Before I got in, I saw a stand selling these lovely wrist bands so, I bought it and ran. Inside the main bit of the church, Emerly was waiting in a room near the back of the church, she must have thought that i wasn't going to turn up then suddenly I came into the church. I looked around then ran to the front of the church and that was that my meeting with the register and the priest would take place later as I arrived very late. During the ceremony, I gave Emerly the wrist band and it made a bit happier and I suppose also she was relieved that I turned up. I definitely shouldn't have left it so late as I did. during the service, I looked around and I thought I was dreaming but I thought I saw a tear come down from my dad's face and for me. That was definitely a rare sight. All throughout the service and until the end it was so intense to me and I really felt the nerves but if I felt like that then I could only imagine how she was. All up until the moment we both said I Do it was very nervous. We both had written our own vows and shared them. Standing in front of her saying my vows and listening to Emerly say hers was exceptional when the service was over. We took a lot of pictures and we both enjoyed doing the pictures and love moment. The reception went well, a few speeches were given from both the parents, the best man and the maid of honour, me and Emerly gave ours last as we had talked about it and decided this together as this is what we wanted. The night finished of excellently and on a day where anything bad can happen nothing bad happened and it all went down great.

The Past, The Present, The Honeymoon

That night, my mum got back home the first thing she went into my old room and sat down at the end of the bed. She was thinking about all the good times, the past and the wedding that took place that very same day and with a tear from her eye's she went to bed and fell asleep almost instantly. It must have been late at night in the Canaries when we arrived. All I remember is going to bed and so does Emerly, as it was a very busy day and one of the most important days in my life. The next day, our first day, we went out to enjoy and explore what the Canaries and see what it had to offer. During the day

Emerly began to miss her parents and it was beginning to show. In fairness, she had been with them all her life and I felt the same way about mine so later on, I gave her a hug to comfort her and we bought a postcard. Emerly wrote to them telling them how she felt and to show gratitude. I did mine the next day. We went out to dinner that night to try to relax, enjoy ourselves and of course to have fun together. With so many changes to take place and It was happening very fast. I accepted the fact she missed her parents so that night we talked to comfort her some more. Then I woke up, it must have been a dream or a glimpse into the future and although I'm not sure I look forward to seeing what the future has in store for me.

Printed in Dunstable, United Kingdom